Daniel Plays Ball

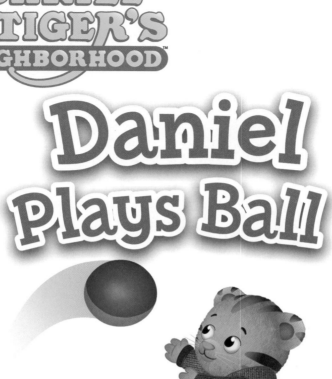

adapted by Maggie Testa

based on the screenplay "Daniel Plays Ball" written by

Eva Steele-Saccio

poses and layouts by Jason Fruchter

Ready-to-Read

Simon Spotlight

New York London Toronto Sydney New Delhi

SIMON SPOTLIGHT
An imprint of Simon & Schuster Children's Publishing Division
1230 Avenue of the Americas, New York, New York 10020
© 2014 The Fred Rogers Company
All rights reserved, including the right of reproduction in whole or in part in any form.
SIMON SPOTLIGHT, READY-TO-READ, and colophon are registered trademarks of Simon & Schuster, Inc.
For information about special discounts for bulk purchases, please contact Simon & Schuster Special Sales at
1-866-506-1949 or business@simonandschuster.com.
The Simon & Schuster Speakers Bureau can bring authors to your live event. For more information or to book an
event contact the Simon & Schuster Speakers Bureau at 1-866-248-3049 or visit our
website at www.simonspeakers.com.
Manufactured in the United States of America 0714 LAK
First Edition
2 4 6 8 10 9 7 5 3 1
ISBN 978-1-4814-1709-9 (pbk)
ISBN 978-1-4814-1710-5 (hc)
ISBN 978-1-4814-1711-2 (eBook)

Hi, neighbor!
We are playing
animal ball.

Whoever throws the ball,

picks an animal.

Then we all make its sound.

You can make

the animal sound too!

Miss Elaina picks a dog.

We all say . . .

Miss Elaina throws the ball to Prince Wednesday.

He catches it.

Prince Wednesday throws the ball to me.

Grr. I missed the ball.

"Keep trying. You will get better," says Prince Tuesday.

"Quack, quack, quack!"

Prince Tuesday throws the ball to Miss Elaina.

She catches the ball.

Miss Elaina throws
the ball to me.

Grr. I miss it again!

"Keep trying. You will get better," says Prince Tuesday.

Miss Elaina throws the ball to me again.

I watch the ball.

Then I hug the ball.

"Nice catch,"

says Prince Tuesday.

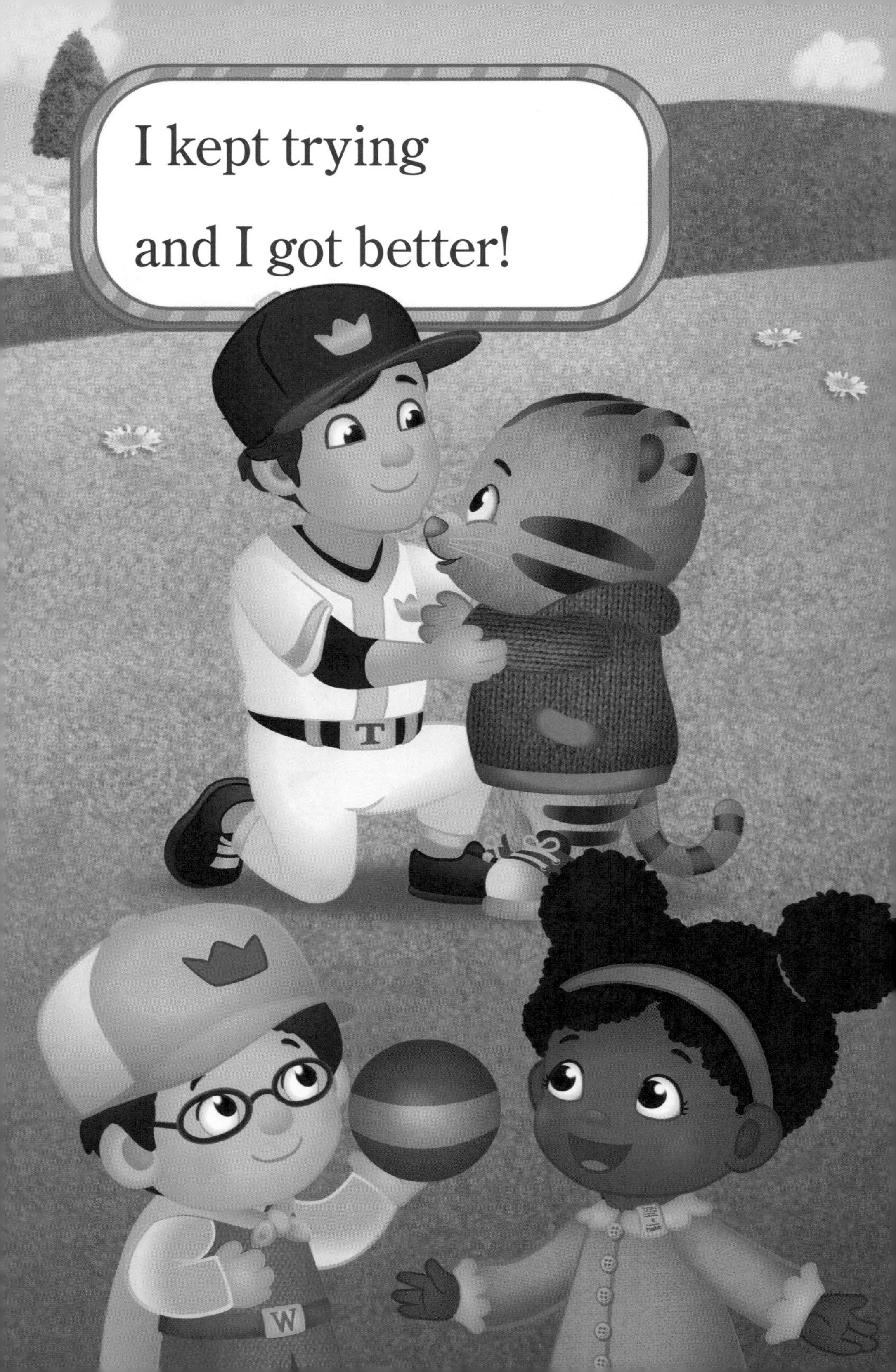
I kept trying
and I got better!

Is there something
you want to do better?

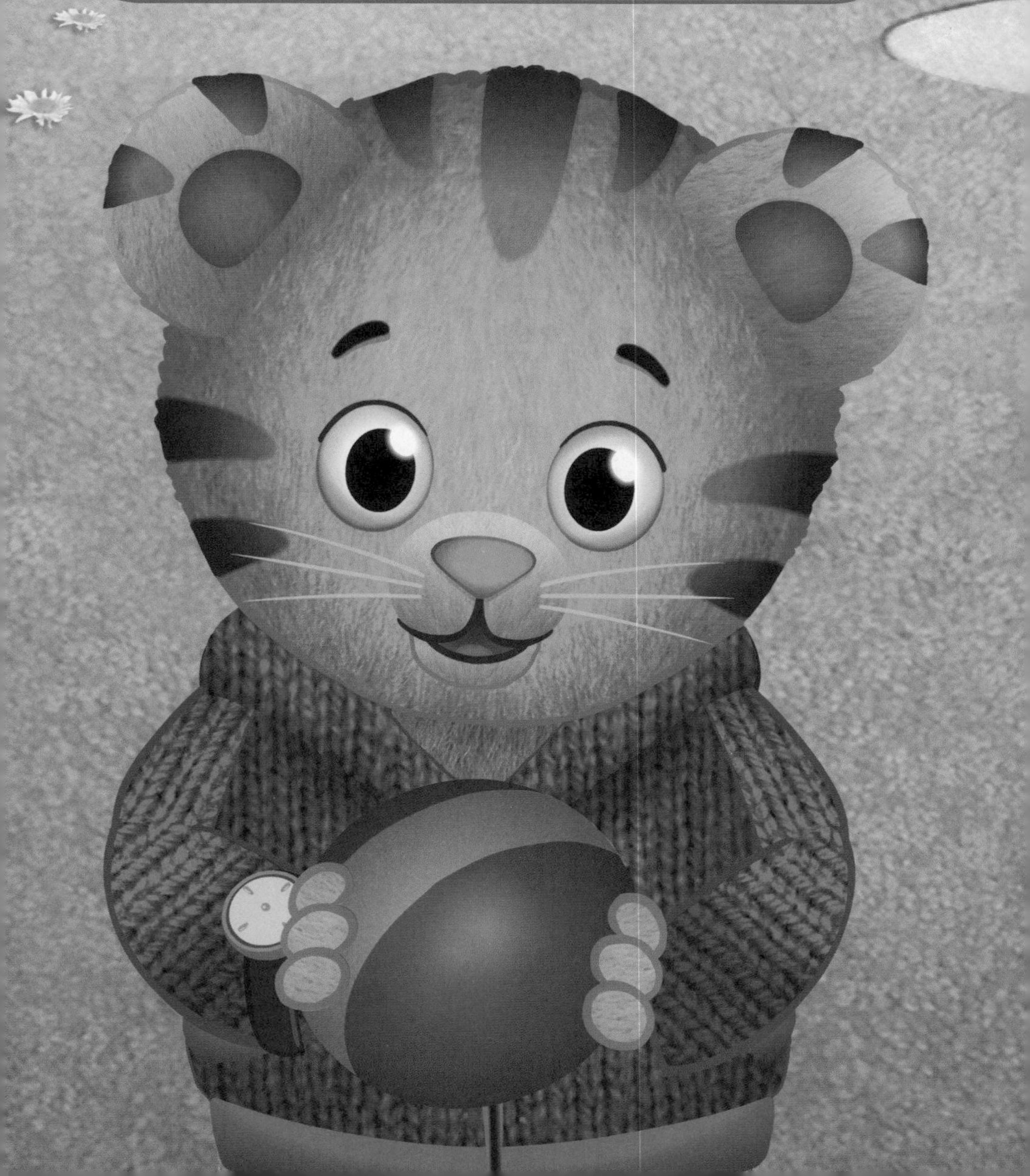

If you keep trying,
you can get better too.
Ugga mugga!